D0053698

Text copyright © 1993 by Alice McLerran.
Illustrations copyright © 1993 by Mary Morgan.
All rights reserved. Published by Scholastic Inc.

CARTWHEEL BOOKS is a trademark of Scholastic Inc.

Library of Congress Cataloging-in-Publication Data available.

ISBN 0-590-44711-4

12 11 10 9 8 7 6 5 4 3 2 1   3 4 5 6 7 8/9

Printed in Malaysia

First Scholastic printing, January 1993

K·I·S·S·E·S

By Alice McLerran
Illustrated by Mary Morgan

Cartwheel
·B·O·O·K·S· ™
SCHOLASTIC INC.
New York   Toronto   London   Auckland   Sydney

Suppose you really like someone —
It feels good just to know it.
It's nicer still if you can find
A way that you can show it.

So you get lots of kisses from
Your daddy and your mummy —

They nibble fingers, nuzzle hair,
And even kiss your tummy.

That seal at the aquarium,
If you could catch his eye,
Might trade you kisses through the glass —
Well, why not? You can try.

Kittens kiss with little licks:
A scratchy kiss, but sweet.

Puppies kiss by licking, too,
But they are not so neat.

Snow on your tongue,

Or raindrops in your hand.

For Eskimos a kiss is THIS:
The reason, I suppose, is
Since they're dressed for blizzards,
They can only show their noses.

The softest kiss of all is made
By fluttering your eyes.
Your eyelashes will make a kiss
That's like a butterfly's.

Some kisses are just wonderful

And some are just all right.

But best of all? That's easy —
It's a snuggly kiss GOOD NIGHT!